Bee My Valentine

By Miriam Cohen

Illustrated by Ronald Himler

Star Bright Books

Cambridge, Massachusetts

Published in the United States of America by Star Bright Books, Inc.
The name Star Bright Books and the Star Bright Books logo are registered
trademarks of Star Bright Books, Inc. Please visit www.starbrightbooks.com.
For bulk orders, please email orders@starbrightbooks.com,
or call customer service at (617) 354-1300.

Hardback ISBN-13: 978-1-59572-085-6
Paperback ISBN-13: 978-1-59572-086-3
Star Bright Books / MA / 00206130
Printed in China / WKT / 9 8 7 6 5 4 3 2

Previously published under 0-688-80129-3 and 0-440-41121-1
Printed on paper from sustainable forests.

Library of Congress Cataloging-in-Publication Data

Cohen, Miriam, 1926-
Bee my valentine / by Miriam Cohen ; illustrated by Ronald Himler.
p. cm.
Summary: The pupils of a first grade class prepare for their St. Valentine's Day party.
ISBN 978-1-59572-085-6 (hardcover w/jacket : alk. paper) --
ISBN 978-1-59572-086-3 (pbk. : alk.paper)
[1. Valentine's Day--Fiction. 2. Schools--Fiction.] I. Himler, Ronald, ill. II. Title.
PZ7.C6628Bc 2009
[E]--dc22
2008036959

To Pat Greer,
Osceola Hankins,
and
Mr. Ziskind's First Grade

"Valentine's Day is coming!" said Jim.
He was happy.

He really liked those funny cards
with the bear saying,
"I can't bear it
if you won't be my Valentine."

"What is Valentine's?" asked Louie.
He was new in first grade.
"It's the day you try to get
the most cards," answered Anna Maria.

"And everybody says,
'You are my sweetheart!
You are my sweetheart!'"
Willy said.

The teacher said, "On Valentine's Day
we send cards to show we like someone.
*Everybody must send a card
to everybody else in the first grade.*
Then nobody will be sad."

"I'm not going to send a card to Anna Maria,"
Danny whispered to Willy.
And Jim thought,
"I'm going to send two valentines to Paul."

After school Jim's mother said,
"Why don't you make
your own valentines?"

But Jim remembered how his hearts
always came out fat on one side
and skinny on the other.

And he could never make those
little bees with big eyes –
the ones that said,
"Bee my honey!"

Jim rushed to the store.
The other kids were already there.
First they looked at all the candy.
Then they each bought a box of valentines.

Each box was the same and
each box had enough cards in it
for everybody in first grade.

"Ooh, this is a cute one! Will you send it
to me, Jim?" asked Anna Maria.
But Jim was thinking about which cards
he would send to Paul.

At last it was Valentine's Day.
The teacher called out
the names on the cards.

Jim was hoping he'd get
lots of good valentines.
Sara waved a card. "Look!
I got one from Sammy.
It says, 'My two-lips are thine.'"

All the first graders were showing
their valentines and laughing.
They asked each other,
"How many did you get?"

Paul told Jim, "I like the ones you sent me.
I like 'Police be my Valentine.'"
He held up a little policeman on a motorcycle.

Danny yelled, "I have thirteen valentines!"
But some of Danny's cards said,
"To Danny, You are nice, from Danny."
He had sent them to himself.

Jim got twelve valentines.
He kept looking at them.
He loved them all.

"See this one,"
Anna Maria said to Margaret.
"I kept it for myself – because
it was too cute to send."

Some people got a lot of valentines.
Some people didn't get so many.
But George didn't get enough.
He ran and hid in the coatroom
and wouldn't come out.

"Oh, dear," the teacher said.
"I'm afraid everyone did not
send a valentine to everyone
else in the first grade.
What can we do to make
George feel better?"

Everybody tried to think.
It was very quiet except for George.
He was crying in the coatroom.
Anna Maria said, "I'll give him one of
my cards because I have so many."

But George hollered, "I don't want it!"

"I know!" Jim cried. "We can play music for him."
He took out his harmonica and began to blow.

Paul went to the music corner and got the trumpet.
Anna Maria took the kazoo before anyone else could.
Willy got the drum.

Margaret planged the guitar.
Danny bonged the xylophone,
and Louie whanged the triangle.

Sara put a pretty cloth on her
head and began to dance.

Around the room they went.
George came out slowly.
Sammy gave him the bells to shake.
He knew that was George's favorite.

Willy got the paper crown
and put it on George's head.
"Hey, man, you are the king," he said.

"And look who's here,"
said the teacher.
Willy's mother was standing
in the doorway.
She brought cupcakes shaped
just like pink hearts!

Danny ate his right away and then he pretended
Louie's hat was a big cupcake.
He pretended he was eating it on Louie's head.
Everybody laughed and laughed.

Then it was three o'clock.
They all grabbed their coats and their cards.
They ran out calling to one another.
"Happy Valentine's Day, Jim."

"Happy Valentine's Day, Paul."
"Happy Valentine's Day, Willy and Sammy
and Anna Maria and Louie and George
and Margaret and Sara and everybody."

"Happy Valentine's Day!"